SUFFER LITTLE CHILDREN

Suffer Little Children

by

Penny Jones

Black Shuck Books
www.BlackShuckBooks.co.uk

First published in the UK by Black Shuck Books, 2019

978-1-913038-36-6

7
Beneath Still Waters

35
The Changeling

53
Swansong

65
Swimming Out to Sea

83
It's Not Just How Beautiful They Are

95
Waxing

Richard lay awake listening to the sounds of crying, whilst his wife slumbered peacefully beside him. He was always surprised that the sound didn't wake her; that unrelenting, gut-wrenching wail that pierced the night. He didn't move.

The first night he'd woken with a start at the cry, his heart hammering in his chest as he tried to orientate himself in the dark. His mind still foggy from sleep, he'd thought the screaming had followed him from his nightmares; beside him Susan woke and mumbled at him to *go back to fucking sleep*. How she could even contemplate sleeping with the caterwauling that echoed through the thin walls was beyond him. He'd turned on the bedside light, causing Susan to burrow deeper, pulling the duvet over her head and clamping it there with her hand. For a moment Richard worried that she'd suffocate herself, sleeping like that, with the covers wrapped so tightly round her face. But then the crying escalated; its pitch a shrill alarm stabbing into the night, a sign of danger, or pain – not a normal cry for food or comfort – and all other concerns were forced from his mind.

Stepping into his slippers, Richard shuffled his way out of the bedroom, easing the door closed behind him. He crept down the landing and stood poised, fingers hovering over the door handle. It was strange, he thought to himself as he worked up the courage to enter the nursery – no not the nursery, not anymore, the spare room. It was strange the way their roles had flipped – before he'd slept peacefully, not even remembering the cries that had caused him to pull the pillows over his head as he slept. It was he who would wake refreshed in the morning to see Susan's red-veined eyes and gaunt skin, bruised by lack of sleep. It was Susan who would wake, who said that she didn't know how he could sleep through the cries and screams. Before it was him who told her that she was over-reacting, that she should ignore it, that the noise wasn't that bad, that she shouldn't go running in every time she heard the slightest whimper. That she should wake him instead to go, maybe take a Nytol or something to help her sleep. Before it was Susan who would wake to the sounds of Amy's cries, but that was before, before the pain, and the recriminations, before the daytime silences and the guilt. Now it was him that woke nightly, unable to sleep through the piercing screams.

~

Richard turned on the tap and filled the kettle, setting it on the stove to boil. Above him he heard the D.J.'s voice cut off in mid-sentence as Susan switched off the alarm. He counted the seconds as he waited for the kettle to boil. The toilet flushed, he picked up three teabags – one for her, one for him, and one for the pot. The toaster popped as he heard the top stair creaking. He opened the butter dish and slavered the fresh toast with butter, each golden swipe in his mind coincided with a stroke of the brush through her blonde hair. He placed the toast on the table mat, at the seat behind him, the one facing the door – Susan hated the seat facing the window in the morning, saying the sun that early hurt her eyes, making her squint and ruining the make-up she'd so carefully applied. He poured the tea into her mug as Susan stepped into the kitchen, placing it on the coaster to the left of her toast, as she sidled into her seat from the right. She picked up her mug and took a sip, grimacing, "It's cold."

Richard reached round her to pick up the mug, but she stayed his hand.

"I'll be late if I wait for the kettle to boil again." She nibbled at her toast before replacing it on her plate. "It's too dry without a drink, I'll just pick something up on the way."

Richard watched as Susan left without saying goodbye. This morning had been a good day, at least she'd spoken to him. It seemed like days could go by in silence, and when she did speak it usually consisted of her screaming or swearing at him.

Richard sat down and picked up Susan's half eaten toast, slowly lifting it to his mouth, he chewed. Unable or unwilling to make himself something fresh, he finished the dry, cold toast, washing it down with the remainder of his tea.

Susan lay on the floor panting like a dog. Richard had to hide the smile that played at the corners of his mouth from the rest of the class. Noticing, Susan uttered a low bark as whale music played in the background. Most of the other couples round the room were intently following the midwife's instructions; the men quietly counting whilst the women lay at their knees, gently breathing. The only other exception was Pat, who had reluctantly come along to the class with her husband. She'd already had one child, years ago when she was a teenager, and said that birth couldn't be that different in your forties. Her GP had disagreed though and had insisted that she attend the antenatal classes.

Susan had asked Pat once how old her first child was. Pat had replied without blinking 'Twenty-one'. But when Susan had tried to continue the conversation over the tea and biscuits at the end of the session, hoping to gain some insight and maybe make a new friend. Pat had clammed up, answering with a shrug and one word – "Adopted" – before hurrying off out of the door. The next week at class Pat had ignored the empty mat next to Susan and had positioned herself next to the midwife.

Susan though was determined. She wanted someone to talk to after the birth, to go out with, and the other mums to be were just that – *mothers*. It was as if since becoming pregnant they'd each shucked off their old persona and stepped into another.

Susan managed to cut off Pat's exit before she bolted from the room at the end of class. Pushing a mug of tea into her hand, she thrust her latest scan picture towards her. "It's a girl. Do you know what you're having yet?"

Pat squinted at the picture, drawing it close as she studied that blurry image "We're having a girl too."

The other child wasn't discussed again. Except for once at their last class, when as they were embracing Pat whispered in her ear – "Don't forget that the birth is easy, it's natural, your body will do all the work. The birth is easy; it's what comes afterwards that's hard" – before gripping her husband's hand and leaving.

A couple of months later the new parents had a get together to celebrate the births. Pat wasn't there, and Susan's heart had dropped. She hadn't really wanted to go – Richard had forced her into the shower and out of the house. She was so tired, she'd have preferred to just crawl into the bath and allow the warm water to gently bob her to sleep. But she'd consoled herself with the thought that at least she'd get to see Pat, maybe swap numbers. Maybe it would help if she had someone to talk to who knew what she was going through. Richard tried to understand, but he hadn't pushed a small human the size of a watermelon out of his fanny. She wanted to do nothing more than crawl away and die, everything hurt. When she bent over to pick up the baby, she could feel her skin stretching against the old scars from the stitches. She just wanted to talk to someone who understood the pain and the exhaustion, and wouldn't just be all smiles and talk about how the baby was a blessing.

Susan asked around after Pat, but no one had spoken to her since the final lesson. The midwife shrugged and said she didn't know, but the doula was happy to tell all. "Oh yes Pat. She was the one who had her baby at City hospital, wasn't she. And then they transferred her to a *different* hospital." The doula winked. "After what happened the last time, they wanted to be sure nothing went wrong... oh no, nothing wrong with the baby, it was the mother, you know." The doula twirled her finger around the side of her head before snatching a look across at the midwife, who was chatting away by the cakes. "It just takes some women like that, no one knows why, but if it happens with the first, it's likely to happen again."

That night once they'd finally gotten home, Susan slipped off her high heeled shoes – she'd not worn them since months before the birth, and her ankles were now swollen and hot. She placed her feet on Richard's lap, glad to rest for a moment. But as soon as she was settled, the cries started again.

"Shall I go?"

Susan just nodded at Richard, keeping her eyes closed, feeling the prickle at the back of her nose as tears of frustration threatened to break through.

~

Richard stared at his phone's screen. He'd done nothing except flick through Facebook for hours

– he never interacted with anyone on here, never liked or shared a post. If anyone messaged him he ignored it, his account settings permanently set to offline. He never checked his timeline, didn't want to see those photos. It was too painful to see those images that he couldn't bring himself to delete, as if it would be a final betrayal. So instead he waited for Susan to go off to work and sat at the kitchen table secretly flipping through timelines, seeing what the people who used to be his friends were doing or saying. It used to be harder; most of the people on his timeline were well-wishers, those who sent their misplaced sympathies to him instead of to Susan, who was the person who really deserved them. Though there were a few who were angry, threatening. Those messages tended to be direct to him, rather than publicly on his timeline, so he could have just ignored them, but he didn't, he wanted to know what people thought of him, really, when they weren't just giving out empty condolences. That anger was what he really deserved. He only ever used his phone for Facebook, didn't even ever take it out with him. No one called him since he'd changed the number. He'd told Susan that he was being bothered with work calls, even though the GP had signed him off. He felt bad for lying, but he didn't want her to know, not about the shouting, or the threats, or the silences when he answered the phone. So he'd changed the number and only she knew what the new one was. Though she never phoned him anymore, no texts signed with kisses. She barely communicated with him when she was at home – he didn't blame her – so she certainly wasn't going to speak to him when he wasn't around. Richard wondered what Susan saw when she looked at him: a lover, a husband, a father... The doctors at the hospital had said it was important to be there for each other, that they were stronger together, but was that what Susan actually wanted? Did she still want them to be a family, or would it be better for everyone if he just went? Richard placed the phone down on the kitchen table, and grudgingly made his way upstairs to shower and change out of his pyjamas into his day clothes before Susan arrived home from work.

Grimacing as he stepped onto the landing carpet, the fibres cold against his bare skin, Richard felt liquid seep over his toes. In disgust he pulled his foot back and, tottering on one leg, he wiped it against his pyjamas.

Carefully lowering his foot to avoid the damp patch which had saturated the floor, turning the blue carpet black where his foot had been a moment before, he scrutinised the ceiling above, searching for a leak. There were no pipes or tanks up in the loft space. It was empty except for the Christmas tree, the cot, and a small suitcase that contained photos, baby clothes and mementos.

Instead of going into the bathroom for his shower, Richard threw on his clothes and headed up into the loft – dinner would be late, and Susan would probably complain that she couldn't wait, that she was hungry after work and that they'd have to order takeaway, although she was sure they couldn't afford it on the one wage – but better that than allowing whatever was leaking to get worse. Maybe if he caught it early enough he would be able to fix it himself, without having to pay through the nose for a roofer. He also prayed that the leak wouldn't have done too much damage to the suitcase.

~

Richard enjoyed this part of the routine. He'd had a chat with his manager at work and got his hours altered, so he could come in early – he was awake anyway, as Susan got up at five to do the morning feed, so he might as well. This way he got to be home in time to put Amy to bed, and give Susan a well-deserved break, allowing her time to put her feet up whilst he made dinner. Then he'd bathe Amy, before refilling the bath for Susan to have one, whilst he gave Amy her bottle and put her to bed. He didn't mind the cries from Amy each time he set her down in her cot. Susan would stay in the bath, topping the hot up as he paced along the landing gently rocking Amy to sleep.

He'd peeked in once as he passed the bathroom door, and for a split second he'd thought she'd drowned. Her head under the water, eyes closed, so still. His heart rate quickened as he stepped forward, bundling Amy over his shoulder as he reached out with his other hand to pull her out. Amy squalled. A small trail of bubbles escaped from Susan's nose a moment before her head crowned through the water. She opened her eyes, blinking, her face blank, no reaction as he stood there hyperventilating, his arm reaching out towards her, fear etching lines between his eyes and cutting deep furrows towards his down-turned lips. She just lay there watching him, not speaking, her eyes unblinking as they gradually turned pink, where the bubble bath seeped down from her hairline and infiltrated past her eyelashes, like tears in reverse. From his shoulder came a steady low hitching, a repetitive sound like a starter motor on a chainsaw, a noise that was all too common, as Amy filled her lungs in readiness to cry out for whatever it was she now required. The caterwauling cut through the air, drowning out the sound of lapping water, as Richard turned and saw that his wife had withdrawn, her face back under, her eyes shut once more against the soapy water.

~

He'd just managed to stick the pasta on to boil when he heard the thump of Susan's briefcase on the hall floor. Wiping his face with the tea towel – sweat and dust imprinting on it – he stuffed it into the washing machine, slightly disappointed that the grime hadn't left an image, a negative rendering of his face like the Turin shroud. He'd jump in the shower after dinner. Hopefully Susan wouldn't notice the cobwebs that threaded through his hair, turning it grey(er) – he didn't want her to worry. She was always going on about money, about him going back to work, about him getting over it. He'd spent ages in the cramped loft space, but there were no signs of water damage, no lost roof tiles or leaks from the water tank. The loft was bone dry. He'd come down to see if he could find where the water had come from, but there was no sign of any dampness or discolouration on the ceiling, and when he'd checked the carpet there wasn't even a ghost of the puddle he'd stepped in.

~

Richard turned the music up on the radio in the shower, inching the dial little by little, waiting for the moment that Susan would scream at him to turn it down, that it reached all the way downstairs and she couldn't hear the telly over his racket. He hated being in the bathroom now, hadn't used the bath since that night, and only used the shower, loo and sink as quickly as possible, nipping in and out. No reading on the toilet for him, or allowing the heat of the shower to sluice away the stresses of the day – it was purely perfunctory, in and out. The only luxury he allowed himself was the radio, because if the rest of the house always seemed to echo with ghostly cries that only he heard, the bathroom was an anechoic chamber. The absence of sound deafened him as he stood brushing his teeth in the morning, and sat crapping on the toilet before bed. So he edged the volume up on the radio, notch by notch, attempting to drown out the silence that filled the room, judging him, waiting to spill out into the rest of the house.

That night Richard woke to the sound of a hitching breath. He lay silent, waiting, listening, hoping that for once the precursor to tears was his own, or at least his wife's. Silence held for a moment, broken by nothing more than the ticking of the clock, the thrum of the refrigerator, and Susan's shallow, regular breaths.

Careful not to disturb his wife, Richard edged his way out of bed and crept out of the room, easing the door closed behind him, steeling himself to pee without the white noise of the radio. He'd considered earphones, but thought that was a step too far. Playing a radio in the bathroom was normal; having to wear headphones to pee in the night was insane.

The silence in the bathroom was absolute as he stepped over the threshold, not even the sound of the fridge motor broke through the impenetrable absence. His arm out in front of him searching for the light pull, Richard took another step. His foot skidded out from beneath him on the wet tiles, as the cord from the light danced away from his fingers. His small shout of surprise was drowned by the undulating cry of his child.

~

"Could you get me a towel? I forgot to bring one in with me." Richard watched as Amy pumped her chubby legs in the rapidly cooling water. Slapping her hands down against the ceramic base of the bath, she chuckled as water splashed up, turning Richard's sleeve a deep navy against the cornflower blue of the rest of his shirt.

"For God's sake. Stop her."

Amy's lip started to quiver, her body tense, her arms raised above her head, held there as she sat stock still, shocked at the sudden shouting from her mother. The quietness broken, Susan stepped forward brandishing the towel.

"Look at the mess, I ask you to do one thing, and it ends up being more work for me. I shouldn't have bothered." Susan bent forward and swiped at the water that had pooled on the tiled floor. Amy's lip quiver was now joined by a rhythmic hitching of her shoulders, as she reached her chubby hands towards her dad.

"Could you grab me another towel?" Richard grasped Amy's questing hand, enveloping her cold, tiny fingers in his. "She's getting fussy."

Susan stood from mopping the floor and chucked the towel towards him. Instinctively he grabbed at it, loosing his grip on Amy and causing her to topple forwards in the bath, knocking her head against the side, the quivering lip and hitching shoulders now developing into full blown screams.

"She's always fussy." The words came out stilted as Susan's lip quivered, matching Amy's.

Richard wrapped Amy in the damp towel, trying to soothe away her tears, as the bathroom door slammed, muffling the echoing cries that infiltrated through from their bedroom next door.

~

Richard sat silently in the GP's office as the doctor talked at him. A soggy Kleenex sat bunched in his fist from the box on the desk that the doctor had pushed towards him like a talisman. He'd booked the appointment knowing that he couldn't go on as he was, but as soon as he sat down, he realised that he had no way of telling the doctor about any of it. The crying that only he heard, the mysterious puddles of water that seemingly dried up in seconds, it would sound insane. So he'd sat down, and instead of calmly trying to explain what was happening to him, he'd burst into tears.

"You're haunted."

The doctor's voice cut through his thoughts.

"It is common, following events such as yours. Guilt... well it affects us all in different ways. I think it would help if you spoke to someone more qualified in these areas than I am."

Richard picked at the shedding tissue, white flakes peppering his trousers. He nodded without looking up. He could feel the blame radiating off the doctor in waves.

"I'll phone you through as an emergency." The doctor pushed a slip of paper across the desk. "This is their phone number. If no one's contacted you in a week, give that number a ring."

Richard nodded and picked up the paper, trying to fold it without shedding more of the desiccated tissue. He waited for the doctor to say something else, something more. But he'd already turned away, checking his computer.

"Well bye. Thanks for everything." Richard waved the slip of paper as if to indicate what the 'everything' was. His GP just raised his hand in a brief wave of response.

Richard made his way out of the surgery, the whispers of the receptionists following him outside, until he got into the car and shut the door against them. Resting his head against the steering wheel he tried to compose himself. He wasn't sure what he had expected. Tablets maybe, something to help him sleep, something to help him forget. There were probably some old tablets still at home, the health visitor had insisted on Susan going to see the GP following Amy's birth, told her that she needed something, some help. She'd gone along but the GP had only given her the tablets. Susan had filled the prescription and told the health visitor that she was feeling much better; but she hadn't taken any of them, hadn't wanted to risk putting anything into her body when she was breast feeding – she told the health visitor she was pumping and throwing the milk away. So once Susan seemed brighter, the health visitor was happy for her to stop taking the tablets. *Breast is best*, as the health visitor always said in her unfailingly cheerful manner. Once she was gone, Susan would stand in the shower, scrubbing her face with shampoo – she hadn't bothered to buy any more makeup remover since before Amy was born – watching the tinted bubbles disappear down the drain along with her tears.

~

The shrill ringing of the telephone echoed through the house. Not the merry jingle of Susan's mobile, or the soft purr of his, but the harsh, demanding ring of the landline. Richard lay in the bed, his hands pressed against his ears, trying to drown out the sound. He wasn't worried about it waking Susan, disturbing her when she had work the next day. The ringing wouldn't wake her, it wasn't sounding for her, only for him. He'd unplugged the landline months ago, at the same time that he changed his mobile number. Susan had wanted to know how people would contact him, he wanted to tell her he didn't want people contacting him, that was the whole point. The calls were more often than not nothing but a cavernous silence, but that did nothing but compound the guilt he felt every time the phone rang. The Pavlovian response that he got from hearing that bell, the bell that was the cause of all their heartbreak. But no, he didn't tell her that. He knew her response. It was his fault, not the phone's. He couldn't go blaming it, it was nothing more than a plastic box stuffed full of wires. He may as well blame the PPI guy who'd been on the other end of the line, or Susan for sleeping through the incessant ringing that was easier for her to block out than her daughter's incessant crying.

The ringing drilled into Richard's brain. *I'll crush my head if I push any harder.* It does no good anyway, why would it? The sound isn't out there, it's inside, inside his head.

Richard stepped out of the bed and made his way down the landing, the carpet squelching beneath his feet, yielding to his weight, water lapping up over the tops of his toes. *If there really was this much water, the joists would have rotted, I'd have fallen through to the ground floor.* Richard wriggled his toes in the warm water – he still expects it to be cold, though there is no reason why it should be.

The ringing isn't coming from the phone sat on the hallway table downstairs, it emanates from the bathroom. Anger surges through him, "That isn't right." He isn't sure what is right about any of it, but they've never had a phone in the bathroom. That night he'd gone downstairs to answer the phone in the hallway. It was a cordless one, but he hadn't thought to take it with him – no one ever phoned them on the landline. But that night someone had, and it had rung and rung and rung. He hadn't wanted it to wake Susan; for once she was asleep. Those wrinkles that had etched themselves deeper in the months since the birth smoothed as she slept. So he'd only popped downstairs. It had only been a second. A moment away to swear, then hang up on the nuisance cold caller that had interrupted their evening. But a moment was all it took. When he returned upstairs Amy was lying there, still, face down in the bath. The coroner said she'd probably tried to get out on her own and slipped. It was an accident.

It may have been an accident, but the blame still lay solely with him, and he saw the accusation in Susan's eyes before she ever spoke it.

~

"I'll be gone overnight." Susan touched up her mascara in the hallway mirror. "It's not as if I want to, but with only one of us bringing in any money, I can't risk annoying the boss, can I?" Susan slicked her lips with lipstick, the vivid red staining her skin.

"New lipstick?" Richard tried to be nonchalant about it. He wasn't stupid; he saw the new clothes, new makeup.

"Yes I thought I'd better make myself look at least halfway presentable at work." Susan smacked her lips together, pouting as she wiped away some excess that had bled in the corner of her mouth.

Richard just nodded. Susan may have been wearing more makeup than she usually wore to work, and the skirt of her suit may have been a tad shorter, the cut of the blouse a bit lower.

"I don't expect I'll be able to call you tonight. This thing could go on a while."

Again Richard nodded. He didn't ask what *this thing* was. He didn't want to know, part of him even hoped that maybe Susan was having an affair, that her late meetings were actually with a lover, rather than colleagues. He deserved it, and maybe if she was cheating on him some of the guilt would be lifted from his shoulders. He wondered if it would be easier if Susan left. Her eyes – so like Amy's – no longer watching him, judging him. "No problem. Hope you have a good time."

Susan paused, one hand on the door handle, the other gripping her overnight bag. "Good time? It's just work Richard." She twisted the handle, "I'll be back tomorrow." There was no smile, no kiss goodbye, as Susan left, not once looking back as she shifted her bag onto the back seat of the car and climbed in behind the wheel. Not even a cheery toot on the horn as the car sped away down the road.

~

Richard sits in the kitchen, shadows creeping round his feet as the sun slowly dips behind the trees that border the garden. He's not sure how long he's been sat there. His usual routine undone, pointless, the realisation that his daily chores are meaningless. What reason was there to shop or cook food for someone who wasn't going to eat it. Or clean the house, or bathe if there was no one to complain about the mess, or stink of B.O.

He only needs to turn his head to see the minutes ticking by on the clock, but instead he measures the time by the pressure of the hard wooden chair as it presses against his butt. The ache radiating out from a single point on each cheek, until they meet and the pain twists up his spine into a knot of spasming tissue in his lower back. He should move, he knows he should, but the pain is the only thing he has felt today, or for a long time. It is only once the shadows have reached the far wall and the kitchen is dark that he eases himself up. Revelling in each popped joint and spasming muscle, he slowly makes his way upstairs, each step sodden as he walks up the soaked carpet.

The light is on in the bathroom when Richard arrives at the top of the stairs, a thin line punctuating the darkness in front of him. He pinches his skin; gripping it between his nails, he twists, and fresh pain blossoms, but the light is still there, beckoning him.

Richard turns the handle, the door bursting open as if he has pushed it hard, smacking against the wall behind, cracking the tiles. The sound of ceramic raining on the floor is a melody to the beating bass of water flowing into the bath. As he approaches the water stops running. He hasn't had a bath for ages, not since before that night. He doesn't even look at the bath anymore, doesn't clean it. Both he and Susan use the shower. But there is no film of dust atop the water, it is clear and inviting. Maybe tonight he will have a bath, climb on in while there is no one in the house to see him, to find him. He could have a long bath.

The water shimmers as a ripple of ever-expanding circles breaks on its surface, leaving the water torpid in its wake. A distorted image of Amy, her eyes open, her mouth open as she tries to either scream or breathe, both of them denied to her. Tears drop into the maw, barely visible as Amy's legs kick weakly against the enamel. Reaching, Richard's sleeves become sodden as his hands search for what can't be there. His wedding ring glinting in the bathroom light as his hand dips beneath the baby-warm water. His arm fracturing, the water seemingly cutting it in its own series of ever extending circles. An infinity that overlaps the original, where an arm also lays split by the refraction. Susan's wedding ring glints next to his, as her hand holds Amy in the bathwater for a second more, before they both disappear beneath Richard's questing fingers.

Stripping, Richard climbs into the now still water. A long bath seems like a good idea, it'll give him time to think, to decide. Richard slips under the water and waits.

The crash echoed through the house. My breath caught in my throat as I gripped the sheet around me. Fear coursing through me like ice water in the hot and muggy room, sure that the noise had been the sound of a window breaking, or the flimsy back door slamming against the kitchen wall as a burglar, or worse, crept into my home.

Reaching across the bed, I felt for Sarah, my wife, praying that she didn't make a sound, that she'd have her phone on the table next to her, the one that I always complained about her bringing to bed. Although she always rolled her eyes and told me it was set to silent, that it wouldn't interfere with my rest, I was sure that those pulsating screeches that emitted from my computer speakers when she left it on the desk to charge were one of the causes of my current broken sleep. Sure that the electronic waves disrupted your sleeping patterns, and periodically woke you silently, in the same way that the silence a moment before the irritating buzz of the alarm clock shocked me from sleep in the morning. That was if we hadn't already been woken by the screams of Luke, telling us that he was awake and ready for the day – though luckily that was happening less now that he was toddling and out of a cot.

My fingers swept the cool sheets – cursing the black-out curtains, I softly called, "Sarah?" But the house and the room remained silent. Reaching across I flipped on the bedside lamp, but the room remained dark. Hands out I stumbled for the curtains and drew them back against the early morning light, a grey patina falling across the room, exposing the empty bed. Barefooted I silently crept towards the bedroom door, easing it open as I scanned the empty landing, the doors standing open, shadows boiling in the early morning heat. Sweeping my hand across the expanse of my son's room, I felt the light switch beneath my fingers, flicking it, the click loud in the silent house as darkness continued to fill the room. From below another crash stopped me from exploring the darkness any closer. The cacophony followed by a silence almost as deafening, as I waited for either the sound of cursing from my wife, or of tears from my son. I opened my mouth to call out, "Sarah, Luke," sure that the crash must be nothing more sinister than a milk bottle falling from tired hands as Sarah lifted it out of the fridge, or Luke's cereal bowl spilling to the floor as he absentmindedly swept his breakfast aside, gesturing excitedly at his mum about all of the things that he intended to do today. But the silence remained unbroken as I made my way downstairs.

The door to the kitchen was shut as I rounded the bottom of the stairs, and as soon as I saw that the front door remained closed and bolted, it was towards the kitchen that I headed. Images ran through my head, broken bottles, spilled milk, the door standing shut with my wife locked outside in her nightdress as she made her way to the fuse box in the garage, the door standing open with...

My hand rested on the handle as I heard the grinding of broken glass behind me. Turning I made my way into the lounge. My son stood there, barefoot amongst the broken glass and crockery. A vase in his hand; the blue one with dolphins blown into the glass, tiny imperfections dotting the material, adding to the image that the dolphins were real, breathing creatures. "Careful" I tried to call out, but my voice only emitted a hushed whisper as I spoke. As if unsure if I'm telling him to be careful of the glass, not to cut his feet on the sharp, dagger like shards that pepper the carpet; or careful don't drop the vase, it's precious to your mother, your grandma left it to her, it's all she has left.

My son turns to look at me, a smile dimpling his cheeks as he raises his hands. I take a step towards him, mindful of my bare feet on the glass strewn carpet, reaching for his extended hands, his face hidden by the vase before he smashes it amongst the others on the floor.

Anger fills me as my hands snatch at his. But they come up with nothing; as I blink my eyes in the darkened room, slits of light play around my grasping fingers where it escapes from the edges of the curtains. My jaw hurts where I've been grinding it again in my sleep, the tendons tight on my neck as I lower my arms, my fingers spasming as the muscles in my forearms try to relax. On the landing I can hear the *stamp, stamp, stamp* of tiny feet on the stairs, next to me Sarah rolls over and tells me that it's my turn to get Luke up.

~

"Chocky." Luke grins as he sits bouncing on his booster seat, greedily eyeing up the plastic mat in front of him, as if it is Thomas the Tank Engine who will bring him his food. "Chocky."

My hand hovers over Luke's usual sugar laden breakfast cereal as the banging starts. Luke slams his spoon against the stained face of the fat controller, the noise like gunshots in the quiet kitchen. He smiles at the sound and, tightening his fist, he hammers the spoon over and over again, the handle carving lines into the plastic, scarring the fat controller's face.

Images surface: of the vase, of Luke stood, smirking amongst the wreckage of his destruction. And I grab the spoon off him, yanking his arm against the back of the chair as his fingers refuse to give up on his improvised drum stick. His face creases, his eyes big as his mouth wavers – reminding me of a cartoon character. I slam his cereal in front of him – cornflakes – the spoon sticking out of the bowl. He looks at me questioningly. "Chocky?" As if I'm a waiter who's gotten his order wrong.

"No." I turn away as Luke start to cry. "No chocky today." The cries turn to screams of rage as Luke sweeps the bowl to the floor.

~

The room is heavy with the summer heat. I glance across at the alarm clock and see the display says 02.38. I have to get up in less than four hours. Next to me Sarah sleeps on; at least, I presume she does, though I can't see her. She's thrown the duvet off in the heat, and it is bundled between us like a third person in the bed. I flip my pillow to the cool side and roll over, avoiding the neon glare of the clock as it counts down to my alarm. On the landing I suddenly hear the sound of tiny feet running, Luke going to the bathroom. My bladder clenches in reply to the thought; I could just try to ignore it, but maybe I'll sleep better after a piss and a drink of water. Anyway Luke has only just started using the toilet – still wears those pull up pads at night. If I need to clean up an accident better to do it now than trying to sort it in the morning when I'll be rushed and tired. I sit up, waiting for the flush of the toilet, but instead I hear the rush of tiny feet. I won't tell him off. I didn't like the sound of the toilet flushing at night when I was his age either; my parent's tellings-off in the morning an acceptable punishment in lieu of the risk of the witch from my dreams sneaking up behind me as I pressed the lever, the rushing of the water covering her approach as I washed my hands.

The sound of feet slows, but instead of the creak of Luke's bedsprings as he gets into bed again, I hear the thump of him making his way downstairs. He should be in bed, and if he didn't want to sleep he could clean his own mess up in the bathroom.

I creep across the bedroom floor, not wanting Luke to know he's been discovered sneaking downstairs and for him to rush back to the sanctity of his bedroom. I open the door and step out onto the landing, expecting to see his guilty face peeping round the newel post at the top of the stairs, but the tread of feet continues thudding down, step by step, as he manoeuvres his way clumsily down the steep stairwell. I stride across the landing, not wanting to keep quiet now – he's trapped, he knows he's in the wrong. I want him to hear me. Maybe he'll freeze on the stairs, a baluster gripped in his chubby fist, using it to balance as he clambers down the stairs. Sarah'd been worried that he'd fall and get trapped between the balusters once he started to climb over the stairgate. That he'd get his head trapped between them, or catch an arm or a leg in them, snapping his limbs like matchsticks. She'd wanted them covered up, but luckily before I'd had to waste my day off boarding them up she'd seen him carefully stepping down, swapping from hand to hand on the uprights at each step, unable to reach the handrail, his grubby fingers turning the elegantly turned white wood grey with dirt. The footsteps didn't stop though, they continued, determined, swifter than usual. As if Luke was walking down one foot to a stair, rather than the awkward *step, step*, each foot touching each stair, that he usually had to employ to make his slow methodical way downstairs. I hurried down the stairs after him, ready to rip the television remote from his hands and send him back to his room. Banning him from watching the telly should stop his nocturnal wanderings and bring some peace to all of us. No wonder I was having such problems sleeping if I was having to chase after him each night. My foot went down, then out from under me, as cold hard metal embedded itself in my sole. My head crashing down, sliding, each step bruising and battering me until I stopped at the bottom. Luke bent down next to me and picked up his toy car. "Hanks Addy." His mocking tone followed me down into the blackness that crept in at the corners of my consciousness.

~

"Shhh! You'll wake Luke." Sarah glared as I crashed about the bathroom; my alarm had gone off at six, and my head was killing me. I checked myself out in the mirror, but no matter how much I prodded and poked there was no sign of injury, no bruise or lumps, scuffs or blood.

"We'll have to start locking him in."

"Who?" Sarah responded as she grabbed her toothbrush from the shelf.

"Luke."

"Why on earth would we lock Luke in?"

"Cause he keeps wandering round at night."

"He's probably just using the toilet."

"No he was downstairs again last night." Sarah stared at me as she brushed her teeth. "He might break something again."

Sarah spat out the minty foam and rinsed her mouth "What has he broken now? Another bowl?" She glared at me, "If you'd given him his own cereal..."

"No that..." I was about to tell her about the vase, her vase, the one her grandma left her, before remembering that it hadn't happened, that it had been a dream. I turned back to the mirror and examined my unblemished complexion, "...It doesn't matter. I'll get him one of those plastic crockery sets from the supermarket on my way home."

~

Although I was tired, I wasn't looking forward to the weekend. If I timed it right during the week Luke would be almost asleep by the time I got home, and not even up before I left in the morning. Each night there was an excuse, a trip to the supermarket to pick up the plastic crockery for Luke (not the one on the way home, it was too small and bound not to stock them; it would be quicker to head to the one out of town and get it from there), a report that needed finishing, Tony from accounts leaving do. It was with a heavy heart and even heavier eyelids that I finally pulled into the driveway late on Friday night. The house in darkness, both Sarah and Luke in bed. I'd phoned at lunchtime to tell Sarah about the leaving do, and she'd snapped saying that it would be nice if they could at least spend some family time together this weekend. That Luke had been fractious all week, crying, asking for his daddy, wanting to know where he was. I was pretty sure that Luke hadn't even noticed I'd been gone more than usual that week, that it was Sarah who wanted to know where I'd been, but I'd kept quiet and promised that I'd be about all weekend. I gazed at the house, dreading the moment that I had to step inside and climb into the bed, Sarah either asleep or feigning it so she didn't have to talk to me. My eyes drooped and my head nodded. Pulling myself up I cursed myself for being so foolish, scared to go into my own house. Reluctantly I slipped off my seatbelt and stepped out of the car.

Easing the door to, I slipped my shoes off and padded up the stairs. The last thing I wanted was to wake Sarah and face the argument that I knew was brewing. Dropping my clothes into the laundry basket I brushed my teeth in darkness, not wanting even the sound of the fan, triggered by the bathroom light, to disrupt the sleeping peace of the house. Slowly I closed the bedroom door, holding the handle down to silence the snick of the lock as it shut. As I released the handle the room lit up, every light on, the ceiling fan spinning, the radio blasting into life. Then like a strobe it all shut off, leaving grey and silver floaters in my eyes. Blinking, I reached out for the light switch, aware that in that brief second of light the bed had been empty, the sheets rucked and thrown to the floor, so there would be no concern about waking Sarah. But flipping the switch didn't do anything, the room remained dark. *Maybe there's been a powercut, it came back on for a second and then went off again. That could send the electrics screwy.* But why the empty bed, the tossed covers and silent house. Fear coursed its way through me, goosebumps rising like hackles on my neck before creeping down my body and causing my scrotum to shrivel and contract. *It's fine. Luke was probably just scared and came running in. Sarah will have gone to settle him down in his own bed, and has fallen asleep in there. There's nothing to freak out about.* But my heart was still pounding as I made my way across the landing towards Luke's bedroom. If it really was a powercut, then why were the streetlights still on, and why hadn't the eruption of noise and light a few moments ago woken Sarah or Luke. The door to Luke's room stood shut; he liked it open so that he'd get some light from the streetlights if he woke in the night. The lamplight from outside cast my shadow ahead of me, eclipsing the handle as I grasped it, merging with the heavy blackness inside the bedroom as I stepped forward. My foot landed in something wet, the carpet sticky and viscous under my bare feet. Wrinkling my nose, I lifted my foot, holding it as if wounded, wondering at what I'd stood in. "Luke? Sarah?" My voice querulous as my breathing quickened. Shallow breaths that dried my mouth and made me light headed. Greyness started to creep in at the corners of the darkness of the room – a fake dawn caused by lack of oxygen. I tried to slow my breathing, a deep breath taken, held, before I gagged at the smell. The fetid aroma familiar yet alien in context of my son's bedroom. Forcing myself to place my foot back into the damp carpet, I stepped into the room. "Sarah? Luke?"

From behind me the sound of Luke's giggle erupted in the darkness as the bedroom door slammed shut.

Pain lanced through my neck as I whipped it back. The sound of the car horn, still loud in the empty street, echoed in my brain. Trying to stand caused more pain as something dug into my stomach and shoulder, holding me down, restraining me, stopping me from moving. What had got me? Luke wasn't here; he'd been behind the door. Had he somehow knocked me out and bound me whilst I was unconscious? But that was stupid, he was a baby – well a toddler now – certainly not strong enough to overcome me, and how on earth would he bind me? He couldn't even tie his own shoelaces yet, had those slip-on shoes with the Velcro that wouldn't stick because it was matted with sand and playdoh from nursery. In front of me the lights glared down one by one as the house lit up; bedroom, stairs, hallway, porch light blinding me as I sat in my car. The door opened and Sarah stood there in her nightdress, arms crossed, waiting.

"Stop being so snappy." Sarah sat next to Luke, her hand resting on his, her eyes weighing me up. "He didn't do it on purpose, he's a kid, he was just trying to help."

Luke sat, eyes wet, small body hitching. My mobile lay on the table amongst a pile of sodden kitchen roll. "You shouldn't have left it charging next to the sink."

"He shouldn't have touched it. He knows not to mess with it, he's always messing with something."

"It was ringing. He was bringing it to you. He didn't know it was plugged in. It was an accident." Sarah smoothed Luke's face, cooing as she wiped the tears. "I hope you two can get along without arguing for a while." Her eyes met mine, the condemnation in them was easy to read – she may have said *you two* but what she really meant was *you*. "I'm going out." Her voice softened. "Why don't you both do something nice together? I'll bring back pizza for tea."

I smiled as Sarah grabbed her handbag, swooping down to kiss Luke on his head, she squeezed his shoulder, before sweeping out of the room – my goodbye kiss withheld as punishment. Sipping my tea I watched as Luke spooned the last bit of his cereal into his down-turned mouth. His hand quivered as he watched me with huge, red rimmed eyes. The front door shut with a final call of "You two behave." Luke lowered his spoon into his bowl, his eyes narrowing, the corners of his lips curling into a smile which dimpled his cheeks. The sound of the car engine turning over filtered through from the driveway. A grinding of gears as Sarah shifted the car into reverse, before pulling off the driveway. I knew I had to think of something to do with Luke – he wouldn't be pacified by sweets and cartoons on the telly all day. But I didn't want to do anything with him. I was still angry – I realised that my anger was misplaced, that the Luke in front of me wasn't to blame for the antics of the Luke in my dreams. But I was still pissed.

Luke watched me, waiting, as the sound of the car dwindled into the distance. Once the growl of the engine had been covered by the sound of birdsong from the garden, he blinked once, before picking up his cereal bowl, extending his hand and, with a twist of the arm, allowing it to fall to the floor.

Sarah pouted at herself, admiring her new haircut in the rear-view mirror as she checked before indicating to turn left, nearly crashing into a police car which was parked across the cul-de-sac, hidden from the main road by the hedges that rambled across the pavement from old Mrs Potter's house on the corner. The end of her street was painted in a wash of blue and red, as the lights stood spinning atop the silent police cars. Sarah wound down her window as a policewoman approached.

"I'm sorry, but the road's closed." The police woman spoke as if by rote. Bored.

"But my house is down there."

"Oh. Okay. What number please?"

"Seven."

"Wait one moment please."

Sarah watched as the police woman walked away and indicated to a gentleman in a suit, just inside the cordon. The two of them gesticulating madly. Of course she lived down here, it was a bloody cul-de-sac. Why on earth would she be turning into the road if she didn't live here? Reaching across to the passenger seat, Sarah grabbed at her handbag, withdrawing her mobile phone. Its screen remained dark as she pressed the button to activate it – dead. She slipped it back into her handbag as she saw the policewoman hurrying back across towards her. Even if she couldn't get to her house at least they would know what was going on. Sarah smiled in what she hoped was a beguiling manner as the policewoman neared.

"Excuse Ma'am but could you just confirm your full name."

The smile faltered on her lips as she stuttered, "Sarah Perkins... Is there a problem officer?"

"I'm sorry Ma'am, but I'll need you to step out of the car."

"Has something happened to Tom, to Luke?" Fumbling at her belt, her fingers numbed by panic, Sarah shied away as the policewoman opened the car door and pressed on the release for the seat belt.

The policewoman held out her hand, her voice soft, the robotic announcements gone, replaced by a gentler tone. "I'm sorry Ma'am, but I need you to calm down and come with me."

Swansong

There are swans on the brook. It sounds idyllic, like one of those old-fashioned renaissance paintings, or the start of an Enid Blyton book. But the brook is really nothing more than a filthy rivulet, trickling behind Aldi; no one goes there, it stinks, reeks of wild garlic and some sort of weed that smells like piss. But still it beats being at home.

Thank God no one ever comes down this way. I don't think I could deal with any hassle from the kids at school, not even my friends. I just want the quiet, to be alone with my thoughts. It was like bedlam at home again today. It's very quiet here, wish I'd brought something to read though, the latest Stephen King is at home, up high on a shelf, so no sticky fingers can find it. It would have been a bit difficult to have brought it all the way down here anyway, doesn't exactly fit in my back pocket like the copies of the Beano that I used to hide from mum. Maybe I should pretend that these are the Barrens, build a dam or something, like when I was a kid and used to pretend I was Dennis the Menace. I'd always hoped for a dog, was going to call it Gnasher, got really excited a couple of years ago when my mum and dad called me into the lounge, said they had something they wanted to tell me, that they knew I was grown up enough and that I could handle the responsibility. I got so excited, I was sitting still and nodding, trying to act like an adult, but inside I was jumping up and down. I peeked glances round the room – had they already got one, or would I get to choose it. I almost didn't hear them when they told me I was going to be a big brother, I thought *who cares, I'm getting a puppy*. Then I realised – *that* was the surprise; not a puppy but a baby. I didn't know what to say, so I just sort of smiled, left the room and made my way upstairs. Later my dad came in and saw me crying.

"It's okay son, no one's replacing you."

I just looked at him, that hadn't even crossed my mind.

I'm too old for make believe now anyway, I've left it behind with the comic books. I slump down against the trunk of a willow, its fronds dipping into the water. Something digs into my back uncomfortably – I reach behind expecting a fallen branch or twig, but I pull out my catapult, turning it over in my hands. I remember when I got it, begged my parents for it, so I could be just like Dennis the Menace. I thought they'd be dead set against it – well my mum was, but after wheedling and cajoling for several months they finally caved and let me have one, as long as I promised that I wouldn't play with it in the house. I haven't used it for ages, to be honest it was a bit crap. I'd set stones up in the elastic, pull, let go, and then they would flop softly to the ground between my feet. I'd thrown it away in the garage and forgotten about it until today, when Toby was playing with it.

I only did it to stop him hurting himself, but again it was me that took the blame. There he was, cross-legged on the living room floor, toy cars and planes scattered around him. I recognised some of them from when I was a kid; heavy, metal ones, not like the flimsy plastic ones that Toby has now. I crouched down by him, intrigued at where he'd found them all, reminiscing about when I was his age and used to play with them – until my mum heard somewhere that they gave you lead poisoning and took them away. That's when I saw my catapult in his hands, one of the silver airplanes hooked by its wings in the elastic, but he'd gotten it all wrong, back to front. I grabbed it off him before he could shoot the damn thing at his face. Mum would be mad at him for playing with it, and even though I hadn't seen the stupid thing for years, you just know she'd be even madder at me. So I took it off him and that's when it started, the lip went and then the screaming began.

Mum ran in, she had a spot of something red on her cheek, jam I think. She'd been baking and had rushed through. "Toby, Toby are you okay?" She dried her hands on something which looked suspiciously like a pair of pants. "Are you hurt? Quiet. I can't help if you don't calm down."

By this point it was bloody obvious that he was okay, and was just being a brat. He was thrashing about, smashing his fists on the floor, cars and planes flying everywhere. Through the snot and the tears he managed to squeeze a couple of words out "Mark...Cattypult"

Mum just looked at me. "I told you not to bring that *thing* into the house."

"I didn't!" What I really wanted to say was "I told *you* not to bring *that* thing into the house" whilst jabbing a finger at my shithead baby brother. But I bit my tongue. It wasn't my parents fault. They didn't know Toby was going to be like that, no one could know a kid could be that bad.

~

The ground under the willow is protected by the fronds, packed hard and cracked where the roots break the surface, bone dry, not marshy and covered in stingers as it is closer to the brook, here the ground is dead. I try to break the soil, to get to the stones held within, easing at the earth with the toe of my sneaker, before standing and hacking at it with my heel. The impacted ground finally gives way to the looser remnants of rocks beneath. I bend and pick one up, place it in the catapult and pull. The whiteness flies through the air, not like it did when I was a kid, when they just fell at my feet. I hear a splash as the tiny piece of gravel hits the water. I sweep my hand across the soil, allowing my fingers to comb the earth, they select stones, flicking them into my palm, before I turn my hand over and allow the detritus to fall back to the ground, leaving five perfect round pebbles in my hand. Each one is about the size of a marble, but unlike marbles these are perfectly white, bleached, as if I have dug up bones rather than rocks. They're lighter too, almost imperceptible holes pepper the surface of them, they'll fly well. I put them in my pocket, wiping the dust off my hands and onto my shorts as I walk, looking for my target.

It's not long before I find my first. High in a tree is a nest – I aim, hoping to knock it from its perch, see what's inside it, maybe take it home. I could put it on a shelf in my room. I pull my arm back, and let go. The stone flies in a straight line, but it arches and falls well below the nest. I set another, and this time I pull back as hard as I can, flicking the catapult as I let go, trying to get as much power behind it as possible. It hits, the nest wobbles – for a moment I think it's going to stay, that it's too well built, too secure – and then it topples. Something falls out as it turns over and over on its descent. I run to where the nest has landed, still intact I flick it over to see what lies within, but it's empty. Feathers peek out from between woven twigs, the bottom sticky with some kind of goo – like when we had to crack eggs to make fried rice in Home Ec. and I got it all over my hands. I scan the ground for whatever fell out, but unless it's in the ferns and thistles I can't see anything. A crow lands on a nearby branch eyeing me up. I move quickly before it decides I'm a threat.

I continue down the brook, past Aldi and its trolley lying lazily in the water; the sun glints off its metal bars, a magpie takes off causing a wheel to lazily rotate. I salute.

The nettles give way to reeds. It looks as if someone decided to build a crossing here, huge chunks of concrete poke through the grimy water, one, two, three, and then they just stop, right in the middle, too far for someone to jump to the other bank. I hop on them, *uno, dos, tres* and stop. I look down the brook – why did they stop, did they run out of blocks or just energy. I turn and look the way I came and then I see my next target. I quietly bring the catapult up and sight along my arm, I let go and the stone flies through the air.

The swan rears up and the stone misses. Before I can get another rock out of my pocket, the swan lowers it head, extends its wings and charges across the water. I hop across the stepping stones, slipping on the last. Grabbing handfuls of weeds, I manage to drag myself up onto the bank. Head down, I try to catch my breath. I glance behind, hoping that it'll have flown off, but still it comes. So I take to my heels and leg it, through the bin store and past the trolley park. I don't look behind again until I open our gate, praying it won't follow me into the house. But the swan has gone.

I sneak past the shut living room door – from behind it, gunshots and explosions echo, the sounds of Toby's 'quiet' time. He'll be sat on the sofa, one hand propped against his head – fingers splayed across his cheek, thumb in his mouth – the other holding his toy dinosaur tight against his chest.

I make my way across the hall and into the kitchen. I'm starving, what with all the excitement with the swan, and that fact that mum yelled at me so I missed my lunch. I hope she's not in there. I peer round the door – the kitchen's empty, the back door shut, she must be in the lounge with Toby. I pour myself a huge glass of squash and drink it down in one, before pouring another, carrying it as I make my way to the fridge. There's a note saying mum'll prepare dinner when she gets back, that she's popped next door to see Sandy.

I glance at the clock, mum won't be back for a while. I ignore the fridge and sneak some biscuits from the tin instead. I make my way into the living room, licking the chocolate off my fingers, making sure not to leave any marks on the white door as I push it open.

Toby doesn't move, he's covered himself with the sofa cushions, even though he must be boiling under them. I guess it's so he doesn't have to talk to me – as a kid he doesn't really have any good coping strategies when dealing with quarrels.

"Are you in a happier mood now?" I sit in the chair opposite. I don't care if he's gonna talk to me or not, but if he's going to be a booger, then at least I don't have to watch his baby crap on telly. There's no reply. "Well, as you're hiding like a baby under there, you won't mind if I change the channel." I expect the sofa cushions to come tumbling down, maybe with several chucked across the room at me, but still there is no reply, unless you count the sob that emanates from the dark interior of his makeshift fort. I pick up the remote and start to flick through the channels, bright primary colours flick by, but nothing catches my attention, all the shows seem to have stupid puppets on them, or goo and custard pies; baby programmes for kids. Finally I settle on an old Road Runner cartoon.

I move over and sit on the sofa, my weight causing the old springs to sag, the barricade of cushions tumbling. Toby burrows his head between the seats, stretching his stuffed dinosaur over his head; the seams on its arms are starting to split, it won't last much longer. "Hey booger, what's up?" Toby's back continues to heave as he burrows his head deeper. I pat him on the head, his cries intensify. "Didn't hurt! Stop being such a baby." I grab his hair and gently pull him out from between the cushions, tears streaked down his face. "Not talking to me, are you?" He tries to turn his head but I'm stronger and hold his cheeks in my hands, so he pulls his dinosaur down over his face instead, snot smearing over the T-rex's tail. "Hey booger, you're getting boogers on dino". Still no answer. God he can be a little shit – not only won't he talk to me, but now he's even starting to make me feel bad, like all this is somehow my fault. "I know what'll cheer you up. How 'bout I teach you to use the catapult properly. I only didn't want you playing with it cause you don't how, and you'd break it. I'll show you."

He peeks over his toy dinosaur and without smiling extends a hand out to me, palm up, fingers stretched; not the hand of friendship, not yet, but at least it's a response.

"Not in here though, mum'll kill us. We'd better go in the garden."

~

He stands looking up at me, the evening sun hiding his face, his shadow taller than he is.

"We gotta have ammo and a target."

He totters round the garden, his pudgy fists gathering up stones of all sizes, before dumping them at my feet.

"No silly, small ones, they got to fit in here. See."

Soon we have a small pile of pebbles. I pin the edge of a blanket, the one nan knitted me for my christening, onto the washing line. It'll make a good target, rings of colour swirl into the centre.

"I'll show you how to do it first, then you'll have a turn. See, you put the stone in here, then you put it up to your face."

The wind has picked up now, my hair writhes around my face. I purse my lips and blow upwards to clear it from my eyes, not wanting to lose my target now it's sighted.

"Then you draw back as far as you can, and then you let go."

The stone flies through the air, straight for the bull's-eye, but the wind gathers the blanket, tearing it out of the way.

I feel a yank as Toby's small hands reach for the catapult. I pull back hard, causing him to fall on his butt.

"That was a practice, we both get a practice before our proper shot. Go and stand over there and hold the edge of the blanket to stop it flapping."

I pull the elastic back, feel the quiver in my muscles, the ache in my arm, I let go. It misses. Toby falls.

"Toby... Toby?" My voice breaks. I notice a smear of red on his cheek. He must have had one of mum's jam tarts for lunch. "Come on Toby don't be a booger, get up, mum'll kill us. Come on, stop playing around. If you stop now, I'll take you to see something special after dinner. Down behind Aldi. There are swans on the brook."

"There's only one Mr Kipling left."

My mother's voice comes out clipped. I ignore her, pointedly staring out to sea as my stomach growls in hunger. I don't care if there is only one pie left, I don't care about the picnic at all. I was supposed to go to the cinema with Joel today, popcorn and Pepsi were what I wanted. I'd got enough holiday money left to buy my own – though it'd have been nicer to have shared, our hands touching as we snaffled our sweet treat. Always sweet, never salty; you can tell a lot from someone's taste in popcorn.

I hear a click, followed by the gentle sigh of gas escaping as either my mum or dad opens a bottle of beer. I swallow, it catches, my throat feels scratchy and dry. I could do with a drink, but I don't turn round to ask. I can imagine the looks on their faces as they lie sprawled on the mishmash of blankets and mats that they threw down on top of the lumpy shore. I can hear their arid laughter burning through the air, the sound abrasive, like the sand whipped up by the sea breeze that scratches at my reddening face. I lift my hand to my throat, the skin there hot, baked feverish in the midday sun. I wince against the dull aching heat which already radiates against my hand. I know I should sit in the shade for a while, beneath the protective shroud of the umbrella and windbreaks that my father hammered into the beach before piling soft sand around their stanchions. I know I should at least ask my parents for some sun cream, to block out the unrelenting rays; but I'm not speaking to them, so I can't very well ask for it, can I? It'll be their fault if I burn anyway. If they'd let me go to the cinema with Joel, I'd have been in the shade. They should have known enough about the dangers of sun damage not to have brought us to the beach on the hottest day of the year anyway. They're useless, stupid, or they just don't care. Either way... I blink back the tears; there's no point in crying, it won't do any good. Anyway, then my parents will know that they've won.

I scrunch my toes into the hot sand, digging my way deeper until I find the damper layer beneath. Coolness soothes the burning on my soles, as golden grains skitter across the tops of my feet, tickling as they glide away. The cool weight of the damp sand against my skin is blissful.

Of course! I chastise myself – I'm nearly as stupid as my parents... nearly. There is another way I can cool down and ease the burning in my skin a little. Hopefully I can minimise any damage before Joel sees me tomorrow. I don't want to look a puffy, red mess when I see him – not on our last day. It'd be crap if the final memories he had of us consisted of me looking like I'd been dipped in a vat of acid. It's not like that wouldn't make him run into the arms of the next woman he saw, as soon as I got in the car to go back home.

I stand, stretch. My burning skin feels taut as I take my first step towards the sea. My mother calls out, something about lunch and not swimming; though whether it's that she doesn't want me going for a swim on an empty stomach, or warning about waiting for an hour after eating, to reduce the risk of cramps, I'm not sure. But I don't acknowledge her, moving farther away from her bleating protestations.

The waves lap against my feet as I step forward. I stand for a moment, the waves ebbing to and fro, pulling at me, gently tugging at my ankles. The sand, no longer soft and golden, is now cold and muddy. It subsides beneath my feet as the waves steal it away. I think about the signs that warn against quicksand further along the coast on the estuary, though they don't call it quicksand, nothing that exotic, the signs just say Danger Sinking Mud. I wonder if there are traces of sinking mud this far up the beach, seams of it lying beneath the surface of the sand, hidden, waiting for the tide to peel back the layers. People have gone missing here, on this beach, drowned, swept out to sea, never to be seen again. I think of cockle pickers as the sand begins to cover my toes.

I lift my feet from the quagmire beneath, the effort more than I expected. The noise, wet and heavy, sounds organic, like a body expelling gas – I'm glad that Joel isn't about to hear it. Embarrassed I turn to see if anyone else has noticed, but no one is nearby. My family are a distant speck. I can only tell where they are from their umbrella, the bright red standing out against the pale beach like a blood drop, marking them.

I turn away again and, lifting my feet against the sucking sand, I carefully step deeper, placing each one down, allowing a moment between each step to compensate for the pull of the tide, and make my way deeper into the torpid waters.

The sea rises slowly as I wade out. With each step the water creeps higher up my legs. What was initially refreshing is now uncomfortably cold as it reaches the edge of my swimsuit, causing me to totter on my tiptoes to prevent the freezing water from soaking me to my waist. My stomach tenses as the waves dance about my crotch, sending icy fingers up the thin material that covers me, causing me to stretch to my limits, so I'm almost en pointe as I try to avoid its chilling caress. I snap my teeth together to stop their chattering. Anger pushes me forward as I remember the taunts of my brother, the refusals of my parents, the nonchalant shrug of Joel's shoulders as I told him I couldn't see him today. They all pulse through me, forcing the blood to rush quicker through my body, its heat battling against the coldness of the water that envelops me.

I take another step. Determined to brave the frigid waters I go to place my foot flat on the seabed, but there is no base, no ground, no floor. My remaining foot teeters on its toes. For a moment I think I must look graceful, like a ballerina, before I fall. The tide grabs at my body, pulling me forward into the sea's embrace, hitting my stomach hard like a slap, forcing the breath from me. The coldness leaches the burning away, the redness of my face turns pale as the water constricts my chest, freezing the little air that remains in my lungs. I fight against my body's urge to breathe, clamping my lips against the impulse to open my mouth wide and take in huge, gasping, lungfuls of air. I kick my legs. Trying to orientate myself I glance through the water, silt dancing in the beams of light. I can see the shelf I had just been standing on; beneath me an abyss, the sun fading into the depths of the sea. I kick my legs powering myself away from the midnight darkness below and up towards the brighter, crystal waters above me.

I tread water. Trying to calm myself, I take a moment to catch my breath. The water no longer feels cold; though now the part of my body that is above the water feels chilly. Even as I feel the sun drying my skin, goosebumps pepper my shoulders and arms. A chill crawls up my neck where the breeze hits it. I sink lower into the water, allowing the sea's warmth to envelop me. I let it bob me gently along on its current, before I swim out towards the horizon.

I feel the stretch in my arms as I dive through the waves, each stroke feels like an arm raised in defiance against those I've left behind. Glancing back towards land I stop and float for a moment, the shore a distant scar the colour of corpse flesh, yellowing and bruised against the blues of the sea and the sky. Everything looks so far away. My family, even the bright red of the umbrella – which stood out so vividly upon the golden beach – are all invisible from this distance. A moment ago I felt strong and invincible, but now I have stopped, the cold wraps itself round my body. The waves that I had just cut through easily suddenly throw a handful of spray against my face, stinging my eyes and coating my lips in salt. My muscles, a moment ago so powerful as they pummelled the sea's surface, now ache from tiredness. How could it be that only a second ago I felt that I could continue swimming until the horizon became a new land? Now I'm not sure if I even have the energy to make my way back to where I came from.

I strike back towards the beach, fear coursing through me. The waves that before had buoyed me along now crash over my head. Each small drowning saps my energy, wearing away at me, dulling my senses, leaching away at the anger that'd powered my strokes, leaving me tired and weathered like a piece of flotsam. I stop, almost too weary to even tread water. I scan the horizon, but still the coast looks distant and unreachable. I try to catch my breath, waves lap at my face. Encroaching over my chin, they creep into my mouth unless I keep it shut. I try to breathe through my nose but it's plugged with snot and salt water. I try to time my breaths to the lapping of the waves, but still the water coats my tongue. I spit it out. Oh God! I want a drink more than anything else in the world. As I lick my cracked lips, my tongue comes away coated in salt.

I'm not sure how much time passes as I wait there in the waves. I'm sure that someone must notice I'm missing. But there is nothing – no boats, no helicopters circling above. I can't tell if anyone is searching for me on the beach; it looks deserted, but I'm too far out to see properly. It isn't until I start to lose the feeling in my legs – an icy sensation that inches it way up from my toes, like when you fall asleep on your arm – that I realise I need to keep moving. No one is coming. If I want to survive I can only rely on myself.

I flip myself back onto my front and start to swim for shore again. But this time I don't go hell for leather, striking out as if I'm fighting against the sea. This time I'm calmer, Zen-like, measured in my approach. A gentle breast stroke, as if I'm caressing the surface of the ocean, as I let it drift me along in its tide. I'm so relaxed, bobbing along, that I almost feel as if I'm at home, relaxing in the bath. Maybe the sea's like a dog, maybe it can sense fear, if I pretend that nothing is wrong, then maybe it won't attack. Finally I feel the scrape of stones against my shins, rather than the undulating water. The waves break, tossing me against the shelf that edges the shoreline. Gingerly I allow my body to fight against the natural buoyancy of the sea, fearful that once I reject the water's embrace it'll tug me back out again, casting me adrift once more. I place my feet down, tiptoes on the loose shale. Letting the waves gently lift me as I slowly walk forward, concentrating on getting to the beach, I wade through the deep water. My legs ache, but not as much as my arms.

The tide's carried me along, washed me up on a different part of the beach. The ledge under my feet is made up of hard stone now, rather than the soft, giving sand where I entered. Rough, the stones press hard into my soles, their edges sharp. I feel something – a shell, a piece of sea glass, some kind of flotsam or jetsam – slice against my foot. The salt stings it as I walk, water swirling against the wound. A caress against my leg. Instinctively I pull away, struggling to keep my balance; just seaweed, or maybe at worst a fish attracted by the warmth of my blood. But then my ankle is grasped, encircled by a burning frond. I kick out until the grip releases me, though the pain continues unabated. I see it then, floating serenely in the water, and I feel sick as I realise it has touched me with its alien tendrils. I try to run from it, but it's as if I'm in a nightmare, my feet are heavy, slow, as I stumble through water that seems thicker than treacle. Ignoring the pain from my cut foot and stung leg. Ignoring my leaden limbs. I don't think of anything other than the need to get away, to escape, to reach the sanctity of the sand where it cannot follow me. The sea sucks at my legs as I lift them higher, dragging me back, then suddenly the sea holds me no more as I collapse onto the shoreline. Face down I lie. I can hear only the cacophony of the sea, its shouts and whispers as its waves crash and fall, the chuckle of the pebbles on the shoreline as it draws itself away from them. I lie for a moment on the shale, catching my breath, unable to move. The sun beats down, tightening my skin as it dries, burning away every ounce of the sea from my body; the droplets evaporate leaving nothing but pockmarks of salt on every exposed inch of my flesh.

My foot and ankle hurt like a bastard. Looking down there's nothing but a small slit by my heel – tiny, it looks too insignificant to cause so much pain. Blood wells slowly, a red drop soaking into the sand before the tide laps at it and draws it back into the sea – and around my ankle a bracelet of red burns stand vivid against my skin. I stand gingerly – not wanting to put too much weight on my foot – and stumble along the beach, looking for my family. I search for my mum, knowing that she'll have something in her bag to put on the wound, something that'd cool the heat and soothe the pain. I can't see them. I can't find them. Again and again I hunt for them. Hobbling across the vast expanse of golden sand, I pray that my father will see me, that he'll come running down the beach and scoop me up in his arms and carry me to my mother's cooling touch. But there is no sign of them, no mishmash of blankets and rugs, no red umbrella. The umbrellas along this stretch of beach are all sun bleached, the colour of parchment, stretched taut over ancient skeleton frames. I avoid touching them as I walk down the beach, their leathery hides spread wide in the day's heat seem repulsive somehow. Shadows lurk beneath, their occupants crowded under, hidden from the sun. I keep away from the parasols clustered together – light on top, dark below, they look like the mushrooms that grow by the brook at home, where the sewer pipe meets the stream, where our parents warn us not to play. The wind gusts, tugging at their swollen caps, causing their frames to rattle like bones. A damp fetid smell emanates from the closest one. I wonder if I should approach someone, explain that I'm lost – though surely the fact that I've been wandering back and forth for what seems like hours now should be sign enough to them that I need help. But not one person has left their protective shade. Maybe that's for the best. I step back and move away, further down the beach,

The chuckling of the pebbles has faded now, as I move further away from the water's edge. The beach is eerily quiet – not empty, just silent. The only sound I can hear now – distant, behind the sand dunes – is the high-pitched echo of children giggling. I head towards it.

The beach here is busier, protected as it is from the wind and the worst of the sun's heat by the towering dunes which dominate the landscape, looming above those that lie in its shade. As I weave my way through the prone bodies – lying so close to one another that there is hardly an inch of sand to show between the raffia mats and brightly coloured beach towels – I feel them turn their heads, watching me as they follow my passage. But when I look back all I can see are reddening bodies as still as corpses. Books cover their faces, the lurid covers wordless show only slighted images of black and red; glimpses of the death and horror and madness which lie within their bindings. I step carefully over the still bodies until they are behind me. I look back, the books now removed as an ocean of faces stare reproachfully at me for disturbing their slumber, their eyes black as they hold my gaze. I back away, hands held forth in apology as I head towards the dunes. A peal of laughter pierces through the silence causing their heads to dart as one towards the shrill sound. The sun throws silver daggers across their shadowed lenses, as I head once more towards the sounds of laughter.

The sand is softer at the foot of the dunes, causing me to stumble as the ground shifts beneath me, crumbling away. Sharp blades of grass slash at my wrists as I put my hands out to break my fall, slicing through my palms as I try to halt my descent. I lift my throbbing hands, sand sparkles in the sunshine where it has adhered to the hatched marks of cuts that mar my skin. I wince at the expected pain as I try to wipe away the worst of the mess, but it doesn't hurt as much as I thought it would, my hands just feel numb and gritty. I stop to assess my minimal progress; huge gorges cut into the dunes show where I'd gotten to, but even before I fell I'd only managed to get a few feet up the dune's bank, and now with the avalanche of sand, the face of it is almost a cliff.

The beach seems to stretch for miles, growing as the sea ebbs away. I look again for my family, but they're not there. I don't even know which way they used to be. If I walk along the beach I could be moving closer, or just as easily moving further away. I pick up a handful of sand, letting each grain fall slowly. I wait, gathering my thoughts. The pile of sand grows between my feet, casting long shadows across my toes. The shade of the dunes, once pleasantly cool, is now decidedly chilly. I look up; the umbrellas are all folded, lying empty like cast off cocoons on the shore. The rows of people gone; the only sign of their occupancy are the neat furrows in the sand where they lay. Behind me in the dunes, there is another distant trill of child's laughter; with nowhere else to head I turn towards the sound and step into the dunes once more.

Luckily my hands remain numb as they slip on the grass and the ferns that I haul myself up with. Blood dapples the delicate fronds, though it is getting more and more difficult to see the changes of colour from green to red, as everything is painted in a crepuscular greyness. My whole foot is swollen now, the cut a soft, white puckered line within; my leg wears an anklet of hardening flesh. With every step I can feel miniscule pops of fluid, like bubble wrap – it feels like that at any moment the swelling will split my skin open. But still I climb one more step, grasping at the blades of grass to help me up.

In the distance I can hear something. I hope it's the road. It sounds like cars; though I don't want to get my hopes up, the distant grumbling could just as easily be the laughter of those children again – the ones who like to play hide and seek in the dunes – or it could be the chuckle of the pebbles on the shoreline as the tide turns. There are strange acoustics in the sand dunes, sound travels differently here, bouncing across the hills before sliding into the gullies to be smothered by the all-engulfing sand.

It is late now; the sun burns low on the horizon, steam clouds rising where it touches the sea. I have given up on finding my family; now anyone will do, just an adult, someone with a mobile, someone with a car so I don't have to walk any more, someone with some water. I still head towards what I hope are sounds of traffic, but it seems faded, more distant now than it did before. I stop and turn, listening intently for where the sound of cars is coming from. I head in that direction, but no sooner do I take a step than the sound dissipates, changes, it sounds lighter, more like laughter. The car engines are still there, faint, but the sound of giggling is louder. I still walk towards it, the grass whipping at my tender legs – it doesn't make any difference. No matter which direction I head in now, the sound of the road is hidden under the laughter. I'm starting to think it might not ever have been the road; the roar of engines sounds so much like the roar of the ocean that I'm not sure I was ever heading towards the road anyway. Maybe it was all just a trick, a game for me to play until I'm all tired out from my day at the beach. I stumble forwards and finally I pull myself atop the dune. Maybe from up here I'll be able to see the road, the sea, something. The grass around me whispers as it tells jokes to the giggling children, while in front of me another dune looms. If I can make it to the top, maybe then I'll at least be able to find my way.

I plant my feet beneath me once more and take a deep breath as I start up the next mountainous slope, my world crumbling as with every step I feel the sand slip away beneath my feet.

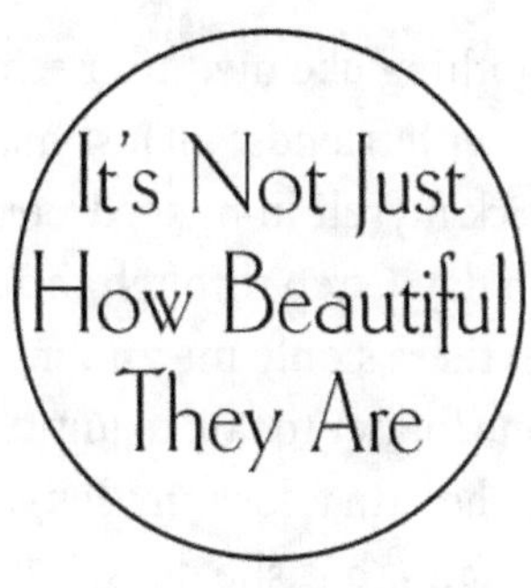

It's Not Just How Beautiful They Are

They're always so mean. Even though they have everything, they're still mean. Even with their perfect hair and their perfect clothes, their perfect grades and their perfect friends, they're still mean. They're not interested in me, in being my friend; they're only ever friends with the pretty, popular, perfect people. They wouldn't hang round with me, they never even notice me, unless of course they're looking for someone to make fun of.

There they go, their noses in the air, their shrill laughter cutting through the thick atmosphere of the schoolyard. Usually that laughter is at the expense of someone else, their happiness growing as it feeds off the misery of others. There they go, making plans – Where should they go? What should they wear? Who's seeing who? And, of course, who *should* be seeing who?

They're nothing like me. After school I won't be going out with friends, I'll just make my way home and lock myself in my bedroom, alone as always. Each day I step through the door into a silent house; there's only me and mum now, so there's no-one for her to talk to until I get home. She says I shouldn't lock myself away from everyone upstairs, but she doesn't understand. It's not her I want to talk to, she's not my friend, she's my mum. The house feels more like a prison than a home, so I stay upstairs, alone, away from her disapproving gaze, and I plan, plan for the day when they'll all finally notice me.

I turn on my laptop and pull up their pages. It was so easy to get them to accept me as a Facebook friend. A false image, a false name and suddenly I can be somebody instead of nobody. In the race to be most popular it's easy for them to just click on my smiling face; accept, accept, accept. If only it was as easy to be accepted in the real world.

I open up other tabs – just browsing, watching, searching for ways to become more popular. In the background the stereo plays the Boomtown Rats; a bit tongue in cheek maybe, but I like it, so have adopted it as my theme song. Sometimes it makes me laugh, but not often. Usually it makes me cry.

Not much going on tonight. Probably because it's a school night and exams are coming up. I start to close the computer down, carefully deleting my browsing history. My mother says she doesn't come into my room, but I'm not so sure, better to be safe than sorry.

It's still light out, I'm not tired but I climb into bed anyway. I toss and turn, waiting for sleep. I need to be up early tomorrow, but sleep evades me. I'll need a clear head in the morning if I'm to get everything ready in time.

The alarm shatters the darkness, a demanding *err, err, err* noise. In my half dreamlike state it sounds like someone's being punched in the stomach over and over again. I used to have the radio set to wake me, but I found that the song playing when I woke would affect my mood for the whole day. So now I just make do with the robotic screams of the alarm, rather than the unpredictable voices of other people.

I sneak downstairs and out of the door before my mum even realises I'm up. She'd only nag me to have a healthy breakfast. In the kitchen, the cupboards are all full of her food, stuff that's full of bran and vitamins. She won't buy the food I like; she says if I want that sugary crap I should buy it myself.

I wait at the end of the road for the bus, glad that I'm out early; at least this way I don't have to share the bus with them. Once I made the mistake of having an extra half hour in bed, and when I caught the later bus it was full. The only seat left was next to Donna. I sat down, and she just turned, looking down her nose at me, before standing and squeezing past my knees as she made her way out to stand for the rest of the twenty minute journey. This way is better, this way is less embarrassing.

As I make my way off the bus I can smell McDonalds. I glance at my watch, my stomach growling. I know that I shouldn't, that I need to lose some weight, but I'm starving and I forgot to pick up my lunch. Slowly I make my way across the bus depot, towards the high street and the concrete grey façade of the fast food restaurant, the bright red and yellow sign doing nothing to dispel the dreariness of the building. I'm unable to see in through the windows which are fogged from the cold, damp weather; unable to tell who might be inside. I take a deep breath and push open the door, the warmth enveloping me as I step through into the harsh, yellow light of the interior.

"Can I help you?"

I'm startled by the sneering voice in front of me. I'd been looking at the menu board, trying to work out what to have. I'm not used to all the different items, mum doesn't like me eating junk food and as I said, I've put on a bit of weight. I'm about to ask what a McMuffin is, when I realise the man stood in front of me, with a smirk across his face and his cap pulled low to cover the spread of pimples across his forehead, isn't a man at all, he's actually a boy, a boy I know.

"A MmmMcMmmmuffin." I stammer.

"What's the magic word?"

I stand flummoxed, what magic word? Is this another test? A way to show how uncool I am? I close my mouth as I realise I'm gaping at him.

"What?" is all I can utter? I want to ask, What do you mean? What is wrong with you? Why are you so mean? What is wrong with me? Why are you so mean to me?

"The magic word... You know, plleeaassee." He draws the word out sibilantly as if he's a snake, before looking at me in disgust. "It doesn't matter. That'll be £2.69."

I didn't know he'd be here, why's he working on a school day? He was in my class last year and made my life hell. Luckily everyone was moved about and put in new sets ready for the exams this year, and when I sat down at the start of term he hadn't been in my class. Come to think about it, I hadn't seen him at breaks or lunch either. I presumed he was just in another set, but maybe he dropped out, or more likely was kicked out.

I stand awkwardly, not sure what to do while I wait for my breakfast. I just want to leave but that'll look weird and it would soon get round at school; even if he's not going, he'll still have friends there. They probably all pop in on their lunch breaks and get free fries and burgers, eating as much as they want, never having to worry about being too fat.

"Here's your meal."

A tray is jabbed in front of me and I'm forced to take a step back to hold it. I paste a smile on my face, trying to seem nonchalant, as if I haven't recognised him. My mum always says that the best way to deal with bullies is to ignore them. As I walk away I realise that my McMuffin hasn't come with a drink and hash brown as the picture shows; I debate whether to confront him, but instead I silently take my tray to a table in the corner, where I can sit hidden by the giant green fronds of a plant.

The playground is empty as I make my way into the school. I creep through the corridors until I get to the chemistry lab. I try the door, expecting it be locked, and nearly fall into the room as it opens silently in front of me.

"Hello" I call out, "Is anyone in yet?"

Carefully, I make my way back towards the storeroom. I know exactly where to find the bottles I need, and quickly pop them in my bag, praying that they won't be needed for any of the classes today. I move the remaining bottles around to hide the empty spots on the shelf and check that everything is in order before leaving the storeroom. I take a deep breath and open the lab door, my excuses ready in case someone sees me coming out, but there is no-one there; the only sign of life is the whirring of a floor polisher in the distance.

I sneak into my class and shut the door behind me. Not surprisingly I'm the first one there; I slide into the seat behind my desk and hide myself behind my books. The bell rings and soon the room fills as bodies start to occupy the other seats. Everyone ignores me as they turn to chat to their friends – with my head down in my book I can pretend I haven't noticed their dismissal. The bell stops and I look up. *Just another day at school* I tell myself, as I absentmindedly pat the satchel by my feet.

As the day drags on, I keep touching my bag, feeling the bottles within, checking they're still there, that they haven't broken. Every time the classroom door opens, or an announcement comes over the tannoy, I jump. Waiting for my name to be called, sure that someone will have noticed the missing bottles. All I want to do is go home but I have to act normal, no change to routine. As the bell rings for the end of the day I wait for everyone else to leave before standing, my bag cradled in my arms instead of coolly slung over my shoulder.

Tap, tap, tap, I keep caressing the glass bottles through the material of the bag. I know my behaviour is strange but I can't stop myself. I'm sure someone will notice something's wrong. In some ways I hope they do and stop me before I see this through.

Tap, tap, tap, I sit on the bus, the bag on my lap, still gently rapping at the glass, as if sending a message in Morse code. *Help me. Stop me.*

I want to open my bag, but not here, it's not safe, I have to wait. I wish the bus would just hurry up and leave. For once I don't want to hang around the bus stop, hoping that they notice me – today I just want to get home.

Mum's out this evening at one of her many bingo nights – there's a note on the kitchen table as I place my bag down. *Tea's in the oven, veggies are in the microwave.* I turn the oven off and leave the tasteless mush drying in the pan. I'm too excited to eat – if I fancy something I'll grab a jam sandwich or a packet of crisps later. Carefully I open my rucksack and stare at the bottles nestled within.

I sit at the table, the bottles in front of me. I've spread paper out over the table, I don't know if the contents of the bottles are corrosive, but better to be safe than sorry, I don't want anyone to be able to track this back to me once it's done. A funnel sits snugly in an empty Hooch bottle I picked up from the park. I can hear mum's voice, scolding me for bringing that dirty thing back, but I've thoroughly cleaned it before setting it on the table. I carefully mix the contents of the bottles together before topping them back up with water. I'll wipe them down and put them back in the lab before school tomorrow, hopefully no-one will even notice the difference. I seal the Hooch bottle back up and carefully hide it in my bag.

~

All day I sit and watch them. Hoping, praying that they'll talk to me. That they'll give me a reason not to do what I've planned. It was easy to slip the bottles back into the chemistry lab, now all I have to do is wait. I've heard them whining that they can't walk home together, that they've got detention. I smile as I listen to them whinge about how unfair it is, that they've done nothing wrong. My feet tap, tap, tap on the floor as I glance at the clock, willing it to move.

The bell rings, and for once I leave the classroom first. I walk fast, I don't run, I don't want people to wonder why I'm running. Once I'm a safe distance from the school, I glance at my watch, before turning to look at the school again. I'm sure no-one can see me from where I am, but I can see them. I can see her walking towards the gates.

"Hello Donna."

"Oh! Hi Mr Robinson."

"I've got something for you." She smiles as I pass her the bottle of Hooch.

"I always thought you were cool." She unscrews the lid and sniffs. "Doesn't smell like Hooch?"

"It's homebrew."

Again she smiles, that beautiful, bright, fake smile, before she tilts her head back, her delicate neck pulsating as she takes a large mouthful. I catch her as she crumples to the ground. I lift her in my arms. She's light, thin; not fat like me. Luckily mum's out at another one of her bingo nights tonight, so the house will be empty.

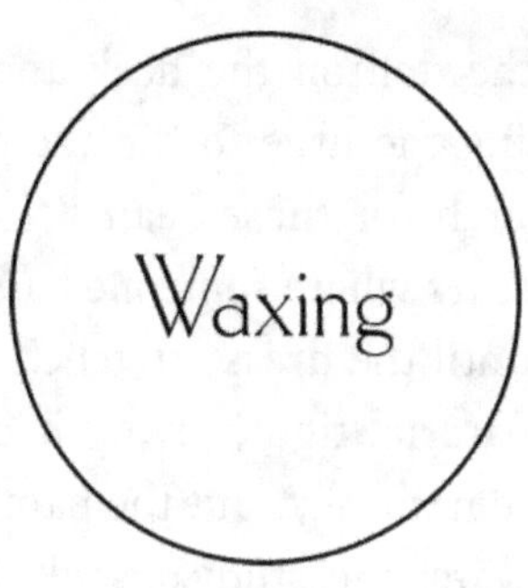

"Would you like to keep it?"

I shake my head, my pigtails whipping sharp against my cheeks.

"But it looks a bit like you. Are you sure you don't want it?"

I turn the doll over and over in my hands, the golden hair turned straw by a thousand brushings, the dress, probably blue originally to match the doll's eyes, now a faded grey from the grubby grasp and cradle of a hundred children's arms. The rag doll certainly does look more than a little like me. The only difference between the two of us is the bulge of stuffing that lies around its middle, stretching the worn material of the dress. I imagine the seams beneath puckered and splitting against the extra padding that lies inside.

"You can keep it you know, at least for tonight."

I place the doll on the desk and cross my arms, fighting the urge to flip the doll upside down to search for those seams, to see those criss-cross scars where someone had stuffed it, bloating it until the dress stretched against its body, the material tight, giving it curves that weren't there naturally. But the painted eyes of the woman watch me, study me still. Those eyes, rimmed black, would narrow as her hand would reach out; elegant fingers, blood red and sharp at the tip would caress my skin. Instead those fingers grasp the doll by the head and drop it on my lap once more.

"Don't you want her?"

Again I shake my head. I want to explain, to tell her how Father would be upset. That when I'd arrived at Hillcrest, Tammy – my own doll – had been taken away. That I was told on entering that I was too old for such toys, that frivolity was a weakness, that to play was a sign of idleness in children and madness in adults. A decadence that would not be tolerated within the house.

"All you need to do is show us... not what he did... just where he touched you."

I stand. I do not speak. I just allow the doll to drop to the floor.

The next day I wake with the sun, the quietness of my room disturbing my slumber. Here I am on my own, no sound of breathing to lull me to sleep or cries in the night to shatter my dreams. On the first night they'd tried to close the curtains, hiding me away from the meagre light of the moon, shrouding me in the room's darkness. But each time they'd snuck in I'd woken, fighting them over the curtains, until finally the rail holding them snapped, the material hanging askew against the window, the plastic thrusting jaggedly like a snapped bone into the room. They removed the rail the same night, and so far no one had replaced it.

I roll over to face the window, to allow the weak sunshine to bathe my face in its warmth. My stomach drops as I turn. Someone had managed to sneak into my room during the night, leaving the ragdoll slumped atop my bedside cabinet. Blue eyes glinting in the early morning sun, its head lolls down, as if staring at the mound of its bloated stomach. I try to ignore the fear that twists in my bowels as I get up, making sure to keep my face blank and my steps steady as I creep my way barefoot into the bathroom. Wondering which one of them had snuck in with their gift while I slept.

I have no names for them, they all look the same to me, dressed in clothes which cut up between their legs and wrap around their chests like a second skin, their faces painted like clowns. When I'd arrived they'd tried to get me to change. Cajoling me, telling me that they only wanted to wash my dress, that it was dirty from the journey, that they would give it back once it was washed. But I'd clutched the material to my body and refused.

Now I wash myself carefully under my dress, in my tiny bathroom, not turning on the light. Making sure that my skin is clean and that I don't smell. That I don't give them any reason to insist on removing my dress and forcing me to put on their immodest clothes.

When I finally emerge pink and shiny, beneath the grey of my dress, breakfast has been placed next to the doll. Its stitched smile smirks as it waits to see if I'll eat today. Most days I don't. I'm pretty sure they're drugging me. Yesterday I caved and ate a fruit pot and drank a glass of water, praying it would be safe. They must have hidden something under the sweetness of the juice, something to deepen my sleep, allowing them to sneak in and place the doll on the table next to me – whether as a taunt or a bribe I don't know.

Picking up the tray I place it against the door; arranging it just so, I put the spoon across the bowl of porridge and stack the metal tumbler of fruit juice atop. My hands hover until I'm sure that it's balanced, before I make my way back to the bed, grabbing the doll and scooting under the sheets with it. Father's warnings echo in my head, reminding me of their false eyes and ears that are always there – hidden, spying, waiting to catch you out, to lead you astray. I'm pretty sure they can't see me under here. They'll know that I've got the doll, that they've piqued my interest with it. But they'll have no idea what I'm doing with it.

Hopefully when I get back to Father he'll be proud that I'm remembering all my lessons. That I'm putting into practice all that he taught me and following the rules. I'm proud of my alarm system too. Now they can't just sneak in and pull the sheets back whilst I'm not watching for them, not without me hearing them at least.

Though maybe *proud* is the wrong word. Father always taught us that *God opposes the proud, but gives grace to the humble,* and I'm pretty sure he meant that pride was something bad.

I push the emotion down deep inside me and flip the doll over in my hands. Running my fingers over the material, so unlike my old ragdolls, the skin feels smooth under my fingers, cool and pliable, like the leather of my old ballet shoes. It holds none of the warmth of the old rough cotton dolls of my childhood. The dress – although made of the same material – is separate to the doll, not stitched to the skin, as if whoever made it expected its owner to dress and undress it. Maybe once, when new, it came with a whole host of outfits, ones that some lucky girl could change it into at her whim; but if so it would have to have been before the doll was re-stuffed, the stomach distended to fill the dress completely. Under the skirt a mark draws its way down the top of the doll's thigh, a purpling which bleeds out from under the tight bodice of the dress. My hand cups my hip as my fingers fan out to cover the birthmark that mars my own flesh. I ease the dress up, inch by inch, wriggling it as I slowly expose the doll's body. The blot could be innocent, nothing more than a careless child's spilt ink, tendrils of it leeching across from the doll's hip, rolling across its stomach before fading along its plump thighs. No one here could know, no one here had ever seen. They tried when I first arrived, tales about a doctor, someone who wanted to make sure I was well, that there was nothing wrong with me. I refused, gripping my dress tight between my legs, told them I was "fine, very well, thank-you very much."

Concentrating on the now naked doll, I can see the myriad of marks. The inked moles and beauty spots, the stitched scars and puckered flesh. My fingers dance over my skin, as my eyes mark each imperfection on the doll's façade. My mind trips back to the fruit cup last night, the sweetness curling in my stomach causing it to grumble in hunger.

~

"If you want to keep it, you must eat."

The doll is clamped under my arm. I no longer let it out of my sight. I even sleep with it under my pillow. I wonder how many girls before me they have tried to drive mad with it.

The marks on the body made as I slept, the rips in the dress as I sat on the toilet, the yellow stains which have leached into the grey material, left there I expect from the minute strands of cotton they have threaded through the seams on the doll's armpits in my moments of distraction. *How could we manage such things?* Their statement becomes a question in my mind. *How* could *they manage such things?* I've stopped brushing my teeth. The toothpaste is drugged as surely as the food they put on my plate. I heard you can go five weeks without food.

I hope that Father comes and gets me soon.

~

My head hurts. I've stopped drinking the water. I was stupid really not to realise. I thought I was so clever, sneaking drinks from the tap in my bathroom, rather than from the glasses that they poured me with my meals, untouched on the trays I had stacked against my door. It wasn't the similarities that caused me to see, to understand, it was the difference. There was only the one, and at first it was tiny, miniscule, a gradual change that would easily be missed by all but the most diligent.

Each morning I would sit in the chair by the window. There was no longer a need to hide beneath the sheets, they already knew that I was on to them. The element of surprise gone, I studied the doll in the bright morning sunshine. Stripping the doll of its dress no longer took the minutes of careful prying and easing of material. The dress now slipped off in one sharp tug from the hem, the material flipping inside out as the collar stuck momentarily on the rag dolls head. I checked the dress – the material was still stiff, hadn't ripped along the seams, there were no visible signs of damage or wear to explain the ease with which the dress had come away. The preceding days quicker inching along the body I had put down to nothing more than that I was becoming more practiced at checking over the doll, my fingers more adept at stripping it back as I came to know each inch of its body. But maybe the answer wasn't in my skill at all, but was only in the natural stretch of a material which had been done and undone a hundred times. I pulled at the dress but there was no apparent give, no sign of thinning or sagging in its leather. I prodded the stomach of the doll, my fingertip no longer finding the hard resistance, dipping the pink leather, the material wrinkling for a second before springing back fresh, no sign of my intruding finger marring its flesh. I lifted the doll to my eyes, the stitching on the seams, still neat and tight, no sign of stuffing poking through. I tried to cover up my discovery, to act normally as I went through the rest of my routine, checking the doll inch by inch, but it was no good, they would know, through their false eyes they would have seen all, and know that I had discovered their latest game.

~

"We need to set up a drip."

They think I can't hear, that I'm asleep. Even without their drugs I can't stay awake now. I'm exhausted. There's no longer any point in not eating or drinking, I'm so weak that I'm asleep more often than I'm awake. My skin now matches the leather of the doll in texture as well as tone. My hands wrinkle as they pluck at the skin to insert the needle, the skin stands proud in ridges, as wrinkled as the now fully deflated stomach of the doll that I hold against my own distended one. I rip the needle out, the tissue paper skin tears along the needle's length, the only act of defiance that I have left.

I want to roll over, but my stomach won't allow it. I've watched it grow fat, even though I haven't eaten for weeks. I don't know how they did it, how they were drugging me. I wasn't eating, drinking, I'd even stopped using the soap and shampoo in case the drugs were leaching into me that way. Maybe it was in the air, blown in through the air vents – I lash out as the women come closer, knocking the doll. It falls against the cotsides that encircle the bed, quickly my hand scoops it up, cradling it against my engorged chest before they can snatch it away. Yes, the air vents is the only explanation, or at least the only one that doesn't sound insane. It doesn't seem to matter now anyway. The knowledge that I did everything I could is the only thing keeping me going. I overheard one of the women talking about Father the other day, apparently he's been locked up. So there's no point hoping that he'll come and rescue me, not if there's no one to rescue him.

"You'll have to restrain her."

The women grab at my arms, leather straps the same pink as the doll's flesh encircle my wrists. Holding me down as they insert another needle into my hand. I watch as the tip punctures the vein that stands prominent as I grip at the doll, my fingers digging into its withered skin. I kick my legs, twisting, as they strap them into stirrups, raised, exposed. My dress puddled around my waist. The weight of my stomach pushing down, the doll snatched away, limp, flaccid, an empty shroud from my grasp, as my fingers curl, the nails cutting into my palms as I push against the pressure. I breathe, I push, I scream.

Acknowledgements

Thank you to Steve Shaw for publishing these stories, to Tracy Fahey and Priya Sharma for reading the early drafts and sharing their expertise with me, to Justin Park and Tracy Fahey for originally publishing 'Swimming out to Sea' in *The Black Room Manuscripts Volume Four*. Thanks must also go to my ever suffering husband Simon Jones who put up with my incessant complaining about writing these stories.

Visit Penny Jones at her website:
penny-jones.com

*Now available and forthcoming from
Black Shuck Shadows:*

Shadows 1 – The Spirits of Christmas
by Paul Kane

Shadows 2 – Tales of New Mexico
by Joseph D'Lacey

Shadows 3 – Unquiet Waters
by Thana Niveau

Shadows 4 – The Life Cycle
by Paul Kane

Shadows 5 – The Death of Boys
by Gary Fry

Shadows 6 – Broken on the Inside
by Phil Sloman

Shadows 7 – The Martledge Variations
by Simon Kurt Unsworth

Shadows 8 – Singing Back the Dark
by Simon Bestwick

Shadows 9 – Winter Freits

by Andrew David Barker

Shadows 10 – The Dead

by Paul Kane

Shadows 11 – The Forest of Dead Children

by Andrew Hook

Shadows 12 – At Home in the Shadows

by Gary McMahon

Shadows 13 – Suffer Little Children

by Penny Jones

Shadows 14 – Shadowcats

by Anna Taborska

blackshuckbooks.co.uk/shadows

9 781913 038366